TH

ESSEN

MUSIC

a manual for composers, copyists and processors

by

SUSAN HOMEWOOD

and

COLIN MATTHEWS

MUSIC PUBLISHERS' ASSOCIATION

LONDON

MUSIC PUBLISHERS' ASSOCIATION
103 KINGSWAY
LONDON
WC2B 6QX

British Library Cataloguing in Publication Data

Homewood, Susan 1958–
The Essentials of Music Copying; a manual for composers, copyists and processors
1. Sheet music. Copying
780
I. Title II. Matthews, Colin 1946–

ISBN 0 9515294 0 4 Pbk

CONTENTS

FOREWORD

The Music Publishers' Association (the MPA) was formed in 1881 to promote and protect the interests of music publishers in Britain.

As part of its efforts to encourage higher standards in music copying and origination, the MPA has pleasure in publishing this manual which is essential reading for composers, arrangers, copyists and processors, and which will be a valuable source of reference to all music students, teachers and anyone who needs to put music on paper or into print.

INTRODUCTION

Even the simplest of copying jobs requires an awareness of many practical details and a large number of rules unlikely to have been learned through the standard channels of music education. This book aims to provide information that will be invaluable to copyists, composers and anyone committing music to paper, particularly music intended for publication.

Beautiful script is less of a prerequisite than many imagine. It is less important to be able to draw the perfect elliptical notehead or the most curvaceous treble clef than it is to know what reproduces clearly and what does not. Many copyists have invested in computerised origination systems with first-class graphics, so need concern themselves far less with the matter of aesthetics than those copying by hand. It is, however, just as necessary for the copyist processing by computer or by any other means to know how to arrange information on a page correctly and with optimum clarity as it is for a hand-copyist.

As well as to have a knowledge of basic notation and graphics it is also useful to be familiar with the idiosyncrasies of notation for different instruments. Provided herein is some useful information on the latter subject, with particular attention given to the somewhat mysterious notation of music for percussion, for harp and for guitar.

Before the content is considered, the copyist needs to know how to lay out a score or part - and even before that (if working by hand), what materials to use. The intended method of printing may limit the copyist or composer to using certain types or sizes of paper, so this needs to be thought about before any other aspect of the copying process. The section on printing and binding begins this volume for that reason.

This book is divided into five main sections. Section I is entirely devoted to practical details, outlining the main printing methods, and gives recommendations for type and size of paper and other essential or helpful equipment for hand copyists. Section II gives guidelines on the copying of full scores and Section III deals with all aspects of the extraction of parts. Notation and graphic style are discussed in Section IV, and Section V shows examples of origination done by various methods.

For advice, suggestions and information we are very grateful to David Bedford, Mary Criswick, Anthony Gilbert, Oliver Knussen, Michael Mack Smith, Simon Mathews, Peter Paul Nash, members of the London Sinfonietta and many others.

Susan Homewood
Colin Matthews
1990

I. PREPARATION

i. Printing and Binding

General

Although these are of course the last stages in producing a score or part, and will be done by a printer, the methods of printing and binding need to be considered before any other aspect of the work, since they may influence the type and size of paper chosen for the original.

If the work is to be published, the publisher will organise the printing and may also supply the paper for the parts copyist to work on. It is, however, advisable for all copyists and composers to be aware of the usual printing and binding methods before they start writing, since difficulties, particularly with full scores, sometimes arise too late.

Scores and parts of less than about eighty pages (that is, twenty sheets) are normally stapled ('twin-wired') in book form, so the printer will need to put two pages adjacently on either side of a double sheet. To allow this, the manuscript will need to be written on paper of conventional proportions (see *Paper*, pages 9–10). If the paper chosen for the original is not a standard oblong of A2* size or smaller, or if the pages are not to be presented in the normal portrait format (that is, with the long edges at the sides), the score will have to be printed on double-sided single sheets.

Single sheets are difficult to bind successfully. Glueing and taping are not strong enough to keep pages together with the kind of use a performing or conducting score is likely to suffer, so, provided the margins are adequate, the best option is spiral binding. This method however is also far from ideal since page-turns tend to be noisy, and after only little use the pages are likely to tear away from the spine. If spiral binding must be used, 'Wire-o' binding must be insisted on, rather than plastic comb binding.

Photocopying

An excellent image will be produced on a good modern photocopier, which may also provide the facility of reduction and enlargement, but paper size and potential binding problems may rule photocopying out as a method of reproducing orchestral parts and conductors' scores. Machines that will

*594 x 420 mm

photocopy in portrait format both sides of an A2 sheet which would be necessary to make staple-bound parts as large as A3* are (at the time of writing) not yet common, and are expensive to use because they cannot be fed automatically.

Photocopies may be produced from a distinct image drawn on any type of paper, but if the original is on a transparency (which is good quality tracing paper, translucent rather than transparent), it should be backed by a sheet of clean white paper which may be taped to the underside of the lid of the photocopier. This will help reflect the light from the un-inked area of the original more effectively, thus minimising shadowing around the printed image.

Copies should always be made on off-white paper since white paper tends to glare under electric light.

Dyeline printing

The dyeline method is suitable for printing both sides of sheets measuring any size up to A1†, so this is a method often used by publishers for reproducing parts and large conducting scores. Opaque white paper cannot be dyelined, however, so the music must be written on transparent paper or, for optimum results, translucent polyester film. Unfortunately, the image produced by dyeliners is not quite so sharp as that produced by photocopiers, and copies will gradually fade with exposure to light, even when protected by a cover. Graphic clarity of the original is therefore particularly important. It is advisable to check that each copy has been printed dark enough; if the image is too grey, it will have a short life.

It is not possible to reduce or enlarge the image during dyeline printing. If reduction is essential or if the original is on white paper, but is too large to make a double-sided photocopy, the original may be photocopied (and reduced) onto blank transparency of the required size, which in turn may be dyelined. By this method, however, the final image will be less distinct than would be ideal, so it is an option best reserved for emergencies.

Offset litho

High-quality printing for commercial publications on a high budget is done by the offset lithography process, which provides a clearer image than any other method, in any size. It is very expensive and therefore unsuitable for the production of performing material and of most full scores to be

*420 x 297 mm
†841 x 594 mm

printed in short runs. If several hundred copies are to be made, however, offset litho is worth considering; the results cannot be bettered and, provided the image is black and dense enough, it is possible to produce copies from any good clear original (though, if it is enormous, not necessarily in its original size).

It should be said, though, that for litho copies, printers prefer originals on white paper rather than on transparency and may impose an extra charge for scores on transparency. Transparency work sometimes produces shadowing on the copy which is difficult to avoid without lightening the image more than might be desirable and, unless an intermediary copy (a photo-mechanical transfer) is made on white paper before the negatives are made, the image may be very slightly blurred. Stave lines on transparency must be thick enough and dense enough; because they are drawn on the back of the transparency and the image will be reproduced as seen from the front, they appear fainter when printed.

ii. Materials

Paper

Ordinary manuscript paper is often used for music which is to be photocopied, or for parts unlikely to be used more than once (such as music for recording sessions), which will not need to be reproduced. Most hand copying, however, is done on transparent paper. This is partly because dyelining was until recently the publishers' standard method of reproduction (and is still the most suitable method for some scores), but also because it is the most convenient form of paper for hand copying.

The greatest advantage of using transparency is that erasure of ink and of superfluous staves is very much easier than it is on ordinary paper. It is important to write the music on the correct side, that is, the opposite side to that on which the staves are printed, to avoid the possibility of accidental deletion of both the music and the staves at the same time.

Paper is available in various sizes. Though proportionately slightly narrower than traditional music page sizes, the most economic sizes to use are the universal A-sizes; this is the range of paper size that all printers stock and which most of their equipment is designed to print on. Standard part paper (traditionally 305 x 255mm) and B4 paper (355 x 257mm) are both commonly used for parts but, if they are printed at actual size on A3 paper (as is most likely), the copies will need trimming, which will add to the cost of production. A-sizes are as follows (to the nearest millimetre):

A4: 297 x 210mm	(turned on its side,	accommodates	2 x A5)
A3: 420 x 297mm	(”	”	2 x A4)
A2: 594 x 420mm	(”	”	2 x A3)
A1: 841 x 594mm	(”	”	2 x A2)

Parts for contemporary works often require a lot of space above and below the stave for symbols and for written instructions, so paper with too many staves will be unsuitable. A3 paper with nine, ten or eleven staves (ideally, all three layouts should be kept) will be most useful for contemporary music. If preferred, however, B4 with eight, nine or ten staves, or standard part paper with seven, eight or nine staves should accommodate most parts.

A 'landscape' format (that is, with the long edges of the page at the top and bottom) may occasionally be preferred for some percussion or keyboard parts and for piano duet music. With a landscape score, however, there are potential printing and binding problems: if it is to be photocopied or dyelined, it will have to be printed on double-sided ('backed') single sheets because the pages are too wide to be printed side by side in pairs on backed double sheets of conventional proportions. Of course, a landscape page will have fewer (but longer) staves, proportional to its dimensions.

Beware of using paper too large to fit on a music stand: the paper should be small enough for the part to rest safely on it and not to obscure the player's view of the conductor or of any other player it is necessary to see. If copying parts for a stage production, remember that the lighted stands in opera-house pits are designed for standard-sized parts and anything larger will not fit on them. Photocopied parts may, of course, be reduced (or enlarged) from the original; but the page size should not be reduced to such an extent that the player has to peer closely at the music!

The size of the stave (that is, the vertical width) is known as the rastral size. The standard rastral sizes are shown on the table opposite. For parts, rastral 1 and 2 are the most useful widths, but manuscript may be printed to order with any number of staves and of any rastral size and with any layout (combinations of five-line staves and single lines for percussion parts, for example). Copyists and composers will find a stock of blank transparent paper very useful in case it is necessary to rule their own.

Transparency should be kept out of direct sunlight, which causes it to curl up at the edges. It is advisable to keep stocks in a drawer or cupboard out of the light since long-term exposure may cause discolouration and

Rastral sizes

Rastral number:	*Vertical width:*
1	(8 mm)
2	(7.5 mm)
3	(7 mm)
4	(6.5 mm)
5	(6 mm)
6	(5.5 mm)
7	(5 mm)
8	(4 mm)

resultant shadows in printing.

For very best results, transparent polyester film may be used. This is, however, very expensive, and cannot be bought pre-printed with stave lines unless specially ordered.

Pens

For work on transparency, it is essential to use a good quality black indian ink designed for technical pens; fountain-pen ink is totally unsuitable since it is not opaque. On white paper, too, indian ink gives the best results. Writing instruments are a matter of individual taste but technical drawing pens such as those produced by Faber-Castell, Rotring or Staedtler are the most widely used for professional music copying. Music pens are not very satisfactory and it is unusual to find one which takes indian ink without clogging. If a flexible nib is favoured, Rotring Graphos pens should be tried, though the range of nibs available is now limited. Old-fashioned 'dip' pens are still favoured by some but it is difficult to obtain nibs of adequate quality for music copying.

If technical drawing pens are used, a collection of nibs in sizes from 0.3 mm to 1.2 mm will be necessary for work on rastral sizes 1–3. For work that is to be dyelined, a 0.4 mm nib should be used for noteheads, stems, accidentals and most other markings; a 0.35 may give a satisfactory image on the transparency or even on a photocopy, but stems, accidentals and bar lines will not show up well on a dyeline copy. The copyist will also need at least three other sizes of nib: a thick one (1.2 or 1.0) for beams (the ligatures joining note stems); one of medium width (0.7) for bold markings such as clefs, time signatures, rehearsal letters and tremolo beams; and a fine one (0.3) for grace-notes and any other delicate details which may appear too large if drawn with a 0.4 pen.

For work on polyester film, technical pens fitted with either tungsten carbide or jewelled nibs will be needed. Special quick-drying ink such as Rotring 'F' ink must also be used.

Erasers

It is almost impossible to remove all traces of ink from normal transparency with an ordinary ink rubber even though the manufacturers may claim it is designed for the purpose; and it will certainly have no effect on unwanted staves. Rotring 'T' Series ink erasers (which contain a chemical to dissolve ink) do work, however, on polyester film.

On transparency, blades are the most effective form of eraser, both for ink and for staves, though it takes practice to learn to use them quickly and efficiently. A razor-blade will do, but a curved scalpel blade on a holder is easier to use. Swann Morton No. 10 blades are ideal. Care must be taken to avoid scraping away too much of the transparency's surface: you may need to rewrite something a second time, but find there is nothing left to write on! Before you write over any area that has been erased, the surface must be smoothed over with a soft india rubber, or with your fingernail.

It is possible to buy electric erasers, but these are prohibitively expensive and favoured by very few copyists. The advantages of these over blades are that electric erasers are gentler on the transparency, so there is less chance of its tearing, and the erased areas do not have to be rubbed over with a soft eraser before being written on.

Extensive errors may (as a last resort) be remedied by cutting the page and taping new staves into place with 'Invisible' or Scotch 'Magic' tape, but try to avoid this if the parts are to be dyelined: the taped areas may show up grey on the copy and, in time, the tape is likely to become detached from the original. The tape should be stuck on the 'wrong' side of the paper, and only where there are no staves or ink markings since the thickness of the tape may cause them to blur in reproduction. Tape should be kept in a box so that the edges do not attract dust. If dirty tape is used, the edges will appear as black lines on the transparency.

Other equipment

For copyists who find it difficult to draw straight lines unaided (that is, most of us!), transparent plastic rulers are essential. Beams and crescendo or diminuendo 'hairpins' are best drawn with a ruler, and many copyists rule stems too. For parts, a 150 mm ruler is most convenient, but for full scores, one as long as 450 mm will be necessary.

If the work is being done on transparency, a helpful guide to the eye is a grid of vertical and horizontal lines drawn on a sheet similar to that being used, placed underneath each page. This is particularly useful as an aid to alignment when writing full scores. Some copyists use graph paper as a backing sheet, but the lines are quite faint and it makes an unreliable guide for drawing leger lines as the grid sizes rarely correspond with rastral sizes.

Blue 'non-print' leads for clutch pencils are available from shops selling drawing office equipment, and are invaluable as an aid to planning bars or for pencilling in a text before the music is spaced above it. Lines drawn *very lightly* with these and, in fact, most blue pencils, will not reproduce on either photocopies or dyeline copies and therefore need not be erased. Ordinary pencils are best avoided for this purpose because graphite lead tends to smear when it is erased from transparency.

Stencils may be found helpful for tempo directions, time signatures and other written information, though the range of typefaces available in stencil is very limited.

Be careful not to get grease on transparency since this makes it difficult to write on. It is a sensible precaution to rest the writing hand on a sheet of paper placed over the lower area of the page. If the writing surface has been spoiled by grease from your hands (or someone else's!), clean the transparency with an absorbent powder designed for the purpose, such as Uno 'Pounce' or Rotring 'Inking Powder'.

Dry transfers

Dry transfers such as Notaset and Letraset are not generally favoured by publishers for the copying of parts, though occasionally professional music processors use them for the origination of full scores or commercial music. Although the finished result, if well done, may be considered aesthetically more pleasing than most hand-copying, the originals will not be very durable: the transfers peel easily and the pages need to be preserved more carefully than inked pages.

There are occasions, however, when dry transfers are useful to the hand copyist; for example the use of Notaset clefs, rather than hand-drawn ones, may give a score a slightly more respectable finish (but see page 48, *Clefs*: two sizes of clef will be required for instrumental parts that change clef). Some publishers may even ask the copyist to use Notaset clefs, though they may dislike the use of dry transfers for anything else.

Application is simple: the sheet of transfers is placed over the manuscript so that the required symbol is in the correct position, then rubbed over with a suitable stylus (it is worth buying one designed for the job) until the symbol is clearly transferred. The waxed backing sheet supplied with the sheet of transfers should then be placed directly over the transferred image and rubbed gently with the stylus. Finally, the image should be sprayed lightly with a proprietary fixative such as Letraset 101 Spray.

II. FULL SCORES

General

If the work is to be litho-printed, the publisher may request that the manuscript be fitted into a certain number of pages in order that the total number of pages should conform to a layout convenient to the printer: ideally a multiple of thirty-two, sixteen, eight or four. This of course includes the inside title page, preface pages and any pages intended as blanks (it is common to have a blank page on the back of the inside title page, for example). Generally, the first music page is a right-hand page, but it does not have to be if starting the music on the left would make for a better layout or more convenient pagination.

The first system of each movement should be indented, with the instruments involved marked clearly before each stave. The traditional order of writing orchestral instruments should be observed unless special instrumental groupings are employed, or unless the relationship is clearly solo plus accompaniment. (Wind quintet layout is often an exception, with the horn appearing above the bassoon.) The instrumentation should be marked in full at the beginning of the score, and wherever it changes. After the first page of each movement, names of instruments are normally abbreviated.

Except in the case of works for small ensembles, where bar numbers alone are sufficient, all scores should contain rehearsal letters (or numbers). These should be put into a small box or circle at the top of each system, and should be centred over the bar line where they will not conflict with any other information. They must be written boldly so that they can instantly be found.

Time signatures and tempo markings should also be bold and distinct. Bar lines should only unite instruments of the same family, unless the work is for wind quintet, in which case the bar lines should extend over a whole system. Straight brackets should be used to show family associations and pairings while curly brackets are reserved for keyboard instruments and the harp.

Score instructions must be clear and the use of too many languages avoided. If the Italian conventions are used, make sure they *are* conventions and are not misspelt or invented. The conductor or performer should not be required to search for a dictionary.

Any unusual notation adopted *must* be explained, either in a footnote at the bottom of the first page where it is used, or else on a separate page of instructions at the beginning of the score. What may seem a convention to one composer because another has used it is not necessarily familiar even to the well-informed reader.

Whether the score is written at pitch with the usual octave transpositions, or with all the transposing parts as the players see them, is a matter of the composer's personal preference, but the method used must be stated. There are strong arguments in favour of both practices, but the two should never be mixed in one piece.

Full scores intended as performing scores

Where ensemble interaction is particularly important, composers occasionally prefer to provide the players with full scores instead of individual parts. This can only be practical in a work for small forces because of the problem of page-turns (see page 23). Where these cannot coincide with rests, the addition to the printed copy of photocopied extracts as appropriate to each part, glued to the ends of right-hand pages or to the tops of left-hand pages, may be the only solution.

Obviously, when a full score is to be played from, all transposing instruments should be written for as played, not in C.

Prefatory information

It is helpful to include in a full score various details relevant to the work's performance.

The orchestration should be listed at the front of the score, with all instrumental doublings given in brackets. Percussion instruments should be listed in detail; if the section is extensive they would best be given a column of their own (or one for each player). If the intended orchestral layout is unusual, it could be shown in a diagram on the same page.

It is conventional also to give the date of composition and details of the first performance (the date, the venue and the performers involved) if this has already taken place. If the work has been commissioned, the commissioning body and the source of funding (if different) should be acknowledged.

If the music pages have any unusual notation that is not explained in footnotes, a glossary of special symbols and any notational idiosyncrasies should be provided in the preliminary pages of the score.

At the foot of the first music page should appear the copyright line, which could be worded as follows:

© Copyright [year] by [publisher/composer/arranger], [town].

Vocal works: text setting and word underlay

Clarity of relationship between text and vocal line is essential. Where there is one note to a syllable, the alignment of all the parts will of course be affected. The words should be sketched in lightly before the notes are added to ensure that enough room is left to write the text clearly. This is particularly important when setting English since there are many 'long' monosyllables such as 'straight', 'through', or 'strength' which, despite the number of letters they contain, may be sung to notes of quite short time-value.

Strictly, syllables (or words) sung to slurred or tied notes should have only their first letter aligned with the first note, if this leaves enough room for the rest of the syllable. Short syllables sung to single or un-tied notes should be centred under the note, but longer syllables sung to single notes should be weighted more to the right: that is, with only the first letter and, perhaps, the second, placed slightly to the left of under the note.

Syllabic divisions are made with hyphens or series of hyphens, so that it is quite clear which syllable goes with which note or notes:

Syllables spread over more than one note (either slurred or tied) have several hyphens, not a continuous line, unless they are single-syllabled words or the last syllable in a word, in which cases their prolongation is indicated by an extended line on a level with full stops and commas, and always *after* any punctuation. The line extends to the beginning of the final notated value (but may be omitted if the written word extends to the same point or beyond it):

No clear set of principles has been established about where divisions between syllables occur. Often they correspond with the divisions used by typesetters of verbal text when a word at the end of a line needs to be split, but concessions are made where the sound of a word could be affected; for example, perhaps ‘sa - viour’ instead of ‘sav - iour’.

A monosyllable should never be split in two just because it happens to be on a melisma: for instance ‘ho - - - - ld’ would be senseless; one has no choice but to sing the consonants at the end.

In vocal parts, only the text should be written beneath the staves. All other indications, including dynamics, are placed above the stave.

Observance of all these conventions is important and greatly helps singers not too familiar with the language of a foreign text. Needless to say, the words should be written in the clearest possible hand, following the punctuation (and choice of capital or lower-case letters) of the author’s original text. The only punctuation that need ever be added, other than that indicating the underlay, is the comma, which is used when the composer wishes to repeat a word or passage, for example ‘It is a beauteous, beauteous evening, . . . ’ (Wordsworth has only one ‘beauteous’).

Modern idiosyncrasies

The excellent system of traditional notation has yet to be bettered, in spite of the occasional attempt to replace it. With the exception of computer-produced or electronic music, there is little Western music that it cannot provide for.

Where the present system is adequate there is little point in making any changes beyond extensions of (or variations on) existing conventions, such as the now widely-used tapered beaming to show accelerando and rallentando:

the use of different-shaped noteheads to represent different tone-colours, and the symbols for quarter-tones as shown on page 43. There can be little advantage, for example, in replacing

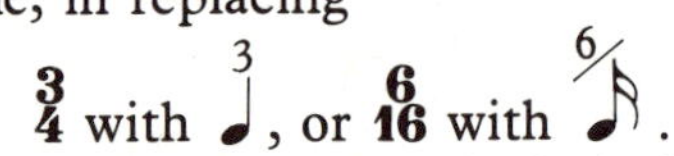

Although these notations may be just as logical, the conventional way of writing time-signatures makes sense, needs no improvement and is immediately recognisable to all musicians.

The composer may feel, however, that always confining notation to what has so far been regarded as conventional has a restricting influence; after all, it is only composers themselves who dictate fashion – or history – by being original. Henze's system, as represented in *El Cimarrón* (1969–70), is admirably logical. The noteheads are central to the stems, thus allowing perfect graphic vertical alignment. Ties are represented by straight lines, as are notes of long duration in unbarred passages (see overleaf).

In a work for small forces, simple and logical notational changes like these can easily be learned by the players. In an orchestral context, though, there is no time to learn new notation. What seems intelligible and logical to the composer, and to a conductor who has spent many hours studying the work, may cause nothing but difficulty for the sight-reading player. It is a fact of life that players have a necessarily practical and pragmatic attitude and tend to be very conservative. There is little to be gained by antagonising the people relied on to present the music at its best.

If new notational ideas are adopted, they should be logical and easily memorised and the explanations *clearly expressed* either in footnotes or in preliminary score pages.

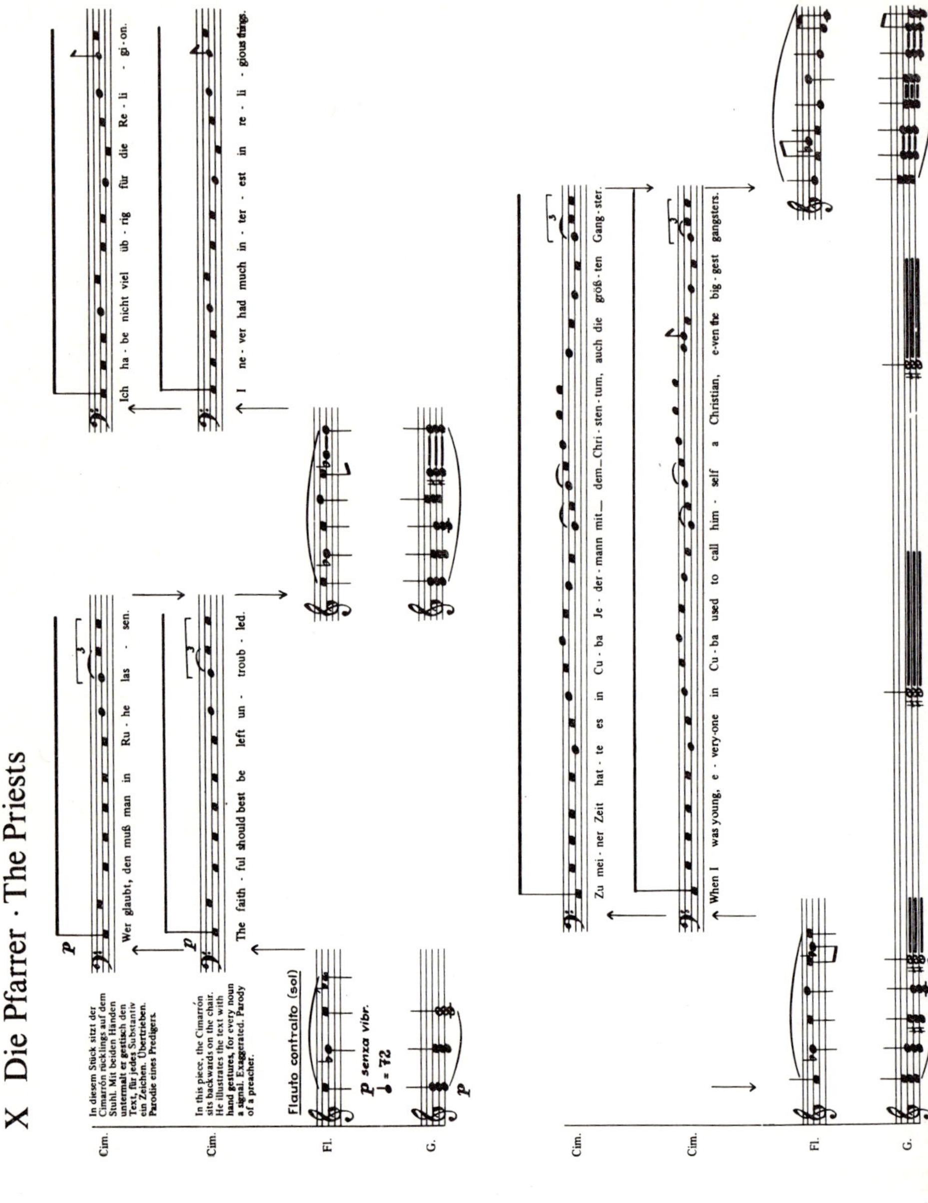
X Die Pfarrer · The Priests
In diesem Stück sitzt der Cimarrón rücklings auf dem Stuhl. Mit beiden Händen untermalt er gestisch den Text, für jedes Substantiv ein Zeichen. Übertrieben. Parodie eines Predigers.
In this piece, the Cimarrón sits backwards on the chair. He illustrates the text with hand gestures, for every noun a signal. Exaggerated. Parody of a preacher.
Cim.
Fl.
G.
Flauto contralto (sol)
p senza vibr.
♩ = 72
Wer glaubt, den muß man in Ru - he las - sen.
The faith - ful should best be left un - troub - led.
Ich ha - be nicht viel üb - rig für die Re - li - gi - on.
I ne - ver had much in - ter - est in re - li - gious things.
Zu mei - ner Zeit hat - te es in Cu - ba Je - der - mann mit_ dem_Chri - sten - tum, auch die größ - ten Gang - ster.
When I was young, e - very-one in Cu - ba used to call him - self a Christian, e-ven the big - gest gangsters.

From the full score of *El Cimarrón* by Hans Werner Henze. This score was hand-copied (with typeset text) under the composer's instruction.

III. FROM SCORE TO PARTS

i. Layout

Pagination

It is a printers' rule that right-hand pages are always given odd numbers, and left-hand pages even numbers. It is preferable to begin on page 1, but the first page may be page 2 if to start on a left-hand page would be more convenient for the layout of the music. If the first page is a right-hand page, do not add the page number; but if it is a left-hand page, it should be numbered so as not to confuse the printer (who may otherwise assume it to be a right-hand page).

The publisher may require that the part should cover a certain number of pages so that the total number is a multiple of four, to avoid unnecessary blanks. This of course must take into account any pages with written instructions and, in percussion parts, lists of instrumentation too extensive to appear neatly on the first music page.

The title of the work and the name of the composer should be written on the first music page, as should the name of the instrument, including all doublings. It is usual to erase one or two staves at the top of the page in order to make room for titles and all such information. For percussion, a complete list of instruments must be given and, if the same part is intended for more than one player, the disposition of instruments among them must be clear. Publishing houses are often particular about how such details are included. The copyist may also be asked to add the copyright line and an edition number.

Subsequent pages must all be numbered and the name of the instrument centred at the top of each page. Right-hand pages should be numbered in the top right-hand corner, and left-hand pages in the top left-hand corner.

Page-turns

Next to the legibility of the music, page-turns are the most important consideration for the copyist; if they are not satisfactorily organised, the publisher or composer will have every right to ask for the part to be re-copied. The whole part *must* be planned in advance; the copyist should never rush blindly into the work and start looking for a possible page-turn when there are only two blank staves remaining on the right-hand page. Nor should the nearest available bars' rest be automatically assumed to be the best turn: there may be a much better place nearby.

Bear in mind that some instrumentalists need more time than others and that percussionists, who are holding and changing sticks and moving from one instrument to another, need more time than most. Always try to avoid page-turns where a player has to change instruments or remove or put on a mute. Since string players sit two to a desk and play from one part, the second player can turn for the first if he or she is not playing at the same time. In many printed sets of parts, string page-turns are virtually ignored for this reason and half the players are obliged to stop playing in order to turn. This should not be emulated!

The best place for a turn is in the middle of a block of rests, though if the rests divide conveniently between areas where the performer's full attention is required (e.g. constantly changing time-signatures) and areas where it is not (e.g. a long passage with rests, followed by a distinctive cue), try to arrange the turn either at the first bar's rest (if this is a suitable point within the piece), or else *before* the place where the player may be able to 'relax' a little – without worrying that he or she has to turn the page before playing again. In general it is better to place rests after the turn so that the player does not see rests at the bottom of the page, but then turn over to find that he or she has to play at once. Turns should not be placed at G.P. bars or at any point where the atmosphere of the music (or the silence) might be destroyed by the sound or movement of a page-turn.

In some cases it may be virtually impossible to plan a suitable page-turn point to coincide with the end of a right-hand page, on account of the given number of staves. Where there is too much music to fit, and similar manuscript with more staves is not available, the lower margin of one or more pages may be trimmed, and an extra stave added to one or more pages taped (on the wrong side) with 'Invisible' or 'Magic' tape.

If there is still too much information to fit, a fold-out or 'flap' page may be used, to make a three-page spread. Flaps, however, can be very inconvenient to the player unless they constitute the first or last page of the part. They should be avoided if possible.

In a contrary situation where there are too many staves for the desired layout and the music cannot be comfortably stretched to cover them, staves which are not required may be erased. If there are only, say, twelve lines' worth of music to cover a left and right-hand page (on eight-stave paper) it is better to erase the top and bottom staves on both sheets and use the middle six staves of each page rather than all eight staves of one but only four of the other.

Spacing

It would be inappropriate to suggest a 'correct' number of bars per line: this will obviously vary according to their content and the general layout. The notes must never crowd one another. Remember that they will need to be particularly clear in fast and florid passages; the player will not have time to identify a squashed accidental or an indistinct dot! On the other hand, badly or over-spaced music is also difficult to read. Musicians have no trouble in coping with ten or more bars to a line in the beautifully engraved nineteenth and early twentieth-century Breitkopf & Härtel editions (see example overleaf), and although there is little contemporary music for which such a close layout would be suitable, the copyist will learn much from studying such judicious use of space.

Within each bar, the notes should give an impression of being spaced in proportion to the beat. This does not mean that accurate graphic proportional spacing is necessary; on the contrary, that would make for over-spaced music and should be avoided. In the example below, for instance, it would be pointless to attempt proportional spacing:

The copyist must beware of unthinkingly transferring the composer's spacing to the part in cases where alignment has caused a disproportional layout in the score, as here:

The bar line must always come at the end of each stave (or system) except where there is a warning time-signature:

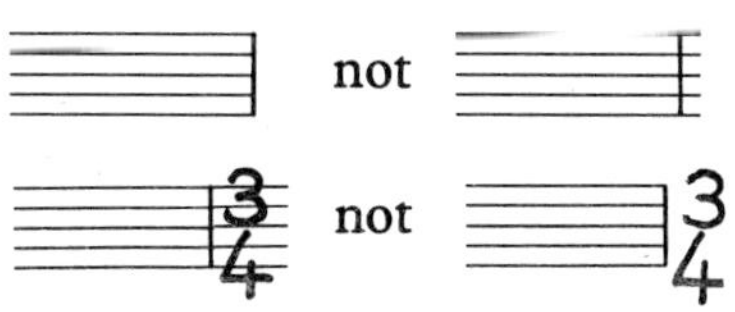

From the second violin part from J. S. Bach's cantata 'Freue dich, erlöste Schar', BWV 30.
Early twentieth-century plate-engraving by Breitkopf & Härtel, Leipzig.

Unless it is absolutely essential, it is better to avoid drawing stave lines beyond the printed width – and also what looks even worse: bars that are split between staves. (In the example shown on page 71, splitting the bar was unavoidable!)

Hand-drawn time-signatures in parts are clearest to the player if they are larger than normal (see above example). This is especially helpful if they change frequently during a piece.

ii. General

Doublings

Composers are notoriously bad at organising the disposition of percussion instruments among players, and may be inconsistent about the usual instrumental doublings (that is, two or more instruments played by one person within the same part). It is the publisher's responsibility to put this right, but the copyist should bear in mind that with woodwind players, unless the composer has a special reason for breaking the rule, the second (of two), or the third (of three) is always the doubling player. If there are, for example, three piccolos, then Piccolos I, II and III will usually be played by Flutes III, II and I respectively.

Changes of instrument must be clearly indicated in the part. For instance, for a flautist, 'take piccolo' (underlined or in capitals or in a box, or whatever the publisher's house rules dictate) should be written just above the stave in the first bar's rest after the flute finishes. As a reminder, 'piccolo' should be written above the stave in brackets where the piccolo begins. The instrument indicated at the top of the page will still be the primary instrument, although the second instrument may be added in brackets.

Multiple parts (parts shared by two or more instruments)

Mutiple parts may sometimes be used for wind and brass players for ease of reading: it can be helpful to amateurs, for instance, to be able to see what the player next to them is doing. The parts should always be written on separate staves except where the instruments play in unison (see *Divisi*, page 44).

Bar numbers and rehearsal figures

If the composer has not numbered the bars of the full score, either the publisher or the copyist should do so. Bar numbers are useful, not only as a reference point for the player, but also to the copyist, to help ensure that he or she does not omit any bars. Traditionally, bar numbers appear above every fifth or tenth bar. This system, however, is often unsuitable for contemporary music since the numbers may obstruct other information placed above the stave. Bar numbers will be least obtrusive, yet most easily found, if they are placed at the beginning of each line, to the left of the clef.

All rehearsal letters or numbers must go into all parts, even where a player has only rests for a long section. They must be written boldly, centred above the bar line and where they will not get 'lost' amongst other information. As in full scores, they should be written in a box or circle to help draw attention to them.

Cues

Cues are essential in music where there is no conductor, and in any music where players have long periods of rest. Elsewhere (if well used) they are more useful than essential. In conducted music, constantly changing time-signatures are a cue in themselves, so instrumental cues are less often necessary.

The addition of cues always needs careful thought; it is not easy to give precise guidelines on what cues should be used where. Where practical, something clearly audible as a landmark should be chosen, even if it appears some way before the actual entry. For example:

would be a better cue than

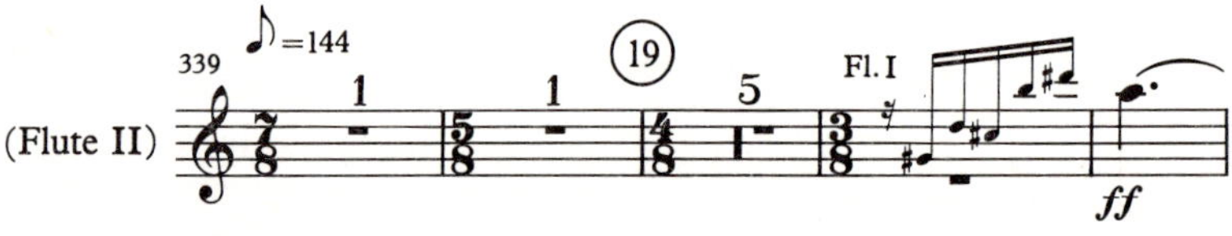

but ideally both cues should be used; the Flute I cue alone gives insufficient warning to the player.

In contemporary music it is often difficult to decide what the player will be able to hear best; sometimes it will be better to give a player a cue from an instrument positioned nearby, rather than from what may seem to be a more important part. With orchestral pieces, the first rehearsals may be sectionals in which the 'important' part may not be playing; this may be an additional advantage to using an instrument from the same group.

The cue should be written in small notes with the stems going in the 'wrong' direction, so that the difference between the cue and the part is immediately apparent. The player's rests will be displaced from their normal position (they should be well clear of the cue – see examples above), but they must be easy to read. Phrase-marks and dynamics should not be included in the cue unless they are particularly significant, or relevant to the main part.

In parts where the main instrument is transposed, cues should be transposed accordingly, unless the player is changing from a non-transposing to a transposing instrument, in which case the cue should remain at pitch. Cues in parts that transpose at the octave should also remain at sounding pitch. When copying from a transposed score, remember to transpose the cues back to sounding pitch where necessary. Instruments of different transposition need careful handling: an alto flute cue in an E flat clarinet part may cause headaches!

Occasionally it may be necessary to place a cue-line on an added stave, for example in free or unbarred sections where the players may take cues from one another while playing. Any rhythmically complex chamber music will be easier for the players if a continuous cue-line is provided (as, for example, in Berg's *Lyric Suite*, published by Universal Edition), but unfortunately this is rarely a practical option because of page-turn problems.

When copying parts for a vocal or choral work, using vocal lines as cues for instrumental parts should be avoided, since it is likely that the singers will not take part in the first (and most important) orchestral rehearsals. Similarly, a soloist's line will be of limited use as an orchestral cue in a concerto, though this does not necessarily apply to works for chamber ensemble with soloist, since the soloist is more likely to rehearse with the group from the start. Where the solo part offers the only available cue it should, of course, be used. 'Cues' indicating that one instrument is to substitute for another (where, for example, a clarinet might be asked to play in the absence of an alto flute) must be clearly distinguishable from normal cues.

Transposition

It is now more common than not for scores to be written at sounding pitch, and it is the copyist's job to transpose parts where necessary. Octave transpositions (for piccolo, contrabassoon, guitar, double bass and some percussion) will, except in rare cases, already have been incorporated in the score. If the composer has indicated this with octave clefs:

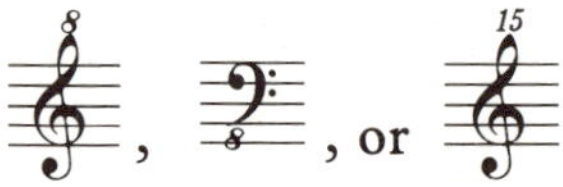

for glockenspiel,

these should be ignored in the part. Straightforward transpositions of the main orchestral instruments are specified in the table opposite; others are explained in the section for each instrument which follows. (See also page 18, *Modern idiosyncrasies.*)

iii. Individual Instruments

Flute

Normal doubling instruments are piccolo (written an octave higher than sounding pitch) and alto flute. The much rarer bass flute, pitched an octave below the flute, is written an octave higher than it sounds.

Flautists, in common with all other instrumentalists who frequently play in high or low registers without changing clef, generally prefer to see their notes at pitch, however many leger lines are needed. The example below, for instance, will cause no problems for the player, whereas an ottava (*8va*) sign might actually make the passage more difficult to read:

It is important to realise that the player translates the graphic position of the note instinctively into a finger position. (Obviously this should not be carried to extremes; in the unlikely event of repeated high C's, the use of an *8va* sign would be preferable.)

Table of transpositions

Instrument:	*Written in part:*	
Alto flute	a fourth higher	than sounding pitch
Oboe d'amore	a minor third higher	" " "
Cor anglais	a fifth higher	" " "
Clarinet in E♭	a minor third lower	" " "
Clarinet in D	a tone lower	" " "
Clarinet in B♭	a tone higher	" " "
Clarinet in A	a minor third higher	" " "
Bass clarinet in B♭ (in treble clef)	a major ninth higher	" " "
Contrabass clarinet	a major sixteenth higher	" " "
Basset horn	a fifth higher	" " "
Sopranino saxophone in E♭	a minor third lower	" " "
Soprano saxophone in B♭	a tone higher	" " "
Alto saxophone in E♭	a major sixth higher	" " "
Tenor saxophone in B♭	a major ninth higher	" " "
Baritone saxophone in E♭	a major thirteenth higher	" " "
Bass saxophone in B♭	a major sixteenth higher	" " "
Contrabass saxophone in E♭	a major twentieth higher	" " "
Horn in F	a fifth higher	" " "
Trumpet in D	a tone lower	" " "
Trumpet in B♭	a tone higher	" " "
Cornet in B♭	a tone higher	" " "
Flugelhorn in B♭	a tone higher	" " "

Bass trumpet in B♭ }
Bass trumpet in C } see page 33: *Trumpet*

N.B. A specialist manual should be consulted for transpositions employed in brass band scores.

Oboe

The oboe doubles with the cor anglais and, more rarely, with the oboe d'amore, the bass (or baritone) oboe and the heckelphone. The two latter instruments are both written an octave above sounding pitch.

Clarinet

The standard instruments are in B flat and in A. The A clarinet is rarely found in contemporary music but all professional players will own one. Doubling instruments are the E flat clarinet, the bass clarinet (in B flat) and the contrabass clarinet (in B flat). The composer will probably have used an octave transposition for the contrabass clarinet (as for contrabassoon) so that, to the copyist, transposition is as for bass clarinet. Although bass and contrabass clarinet parts are occasionally written in the bass clef (and transposed only up a major second), it is preferable always to use the treble clef. The basset horn also uses the treble clef.

Clarinets in D and C, E flat alto and E flat contrabass clarinets, and the basset horn in A are very occasionally used.

Saxophone

All saxophones use the treble clef. In the orchestra, saxophones are usually played by clarinettists but occasionally flautists or oboists double saxophone since the fingering is similar.

Bassoon

The bassoon doubles only with the contrabassoon, which is written an octave above sounding pitch. In high registers the tenor clef should be used for the bassoon, although extended passages may go into the treble clef. Contrabassoons almost always need only the bass clef (although the tenor clef presents no problems of course).

Horns

The French horn is written in F and normally uses the treble clef. Problems arise with low notes written in the bass clef because, in the past, horn parts were written a fourth below sounding pitch when in the bass clef. This practice is now obsolete, but if the bass clef is used it is safest to add a note such as 'horns in bass clef sound a fifth lower'. Safer still is to avoid using the bass clef unless it is essential; horn players are quite happy reading down to C:

If Wagner tubas are asked for, it may be best to consult the players concerned, since transposition has never been standardised. Generally the B flat (tenor) is written (in treble and bass clefs) a major second higher than it sounds, and the F (bass) tuba a fifth higher (also in both clefs). But the players may well prefer the tenor to be written in F as well.

Trumpet

Trumpeters are used to playing in many transpositions. The standard instrument is in B flat, but instruments in C, D and E flat are also common (there are others too). Since the choice of instrument is usually left to the player's discretion, it is best, as a general rule, not to transpose trumpet parts at all unless the composer has already done so. If the trumpet part is a solo part, then the player should be consulted if possible. Cornets and flugelhorns are in B flat. Bass trumpets are in B flat or C. If bass trumpets are to be played by trumpeters, they should be transposed up a minor ninth or an octave; if, as sometimes happens, they are played by a trombonist, they should be written at pitch.

Trombone

Tenor, bass and tenor-bass trombones, with their various attachments or 'triggers', are more of a problem to the composer than to the copyist. None of them transposes, but high notes normally go into the tenor clef. (The third trombone, usually a bass, is less likely to play high, and the tenor clef is not normally necessary.) The rarely used alto trombone is written exclusively in the alto clef; if lower notes are required they would be better given to the tenor trombone. The contrabass trombone is written as it sounds.

Tuba

Tubas (other than Wagner tubas – for these see Horns) are all written as sounding, including B flat euphoniums (although sometimes these are written a ninth higher, like the bass clarinet). *8va* transposition should not be used at all in tuba parts, however many leger lines are needed.

Since it takes a tuba player some time to insert or remove a mute, never ask for this to be done at a page-turn.

Percussion

Ideally, the composer should have organised the percussion part so that the copyist has only to copy it. It is not unknown, however, for a composer to have neglected to organise the distribution of instruments, or even to be unaware of how many players are needed.

Assuming the composer has done his or her job adequately, a decision must be made as to whether the part is to be a single or multiple one. Where possible a player should be consulted. Multiple (or score-form) parts are preferable, if they can be contrived without difficult page-turns. If there are four or more percussion players, two parts will probably be necessary. Timpani are traditionally regarded as a separate instrument (see next section) and therefore usually have their own part.

Separate paper for percussion parts has already been mentioned, and if the players are not changing instruments frequently, single lines for unpitched percussion are preferable to staves. In many cases, however, ordinary part paper will be found adequate.

The usual clef for unpitched percussion is **II** , applied to the line or space on which the instrument is to be notated. It the composer has not already done so, the copyist should try to position the noteheads relative to the pitch of the instruments, as here:

This is not an inflexible rule, but should be followed where possible. Obviously, a bass drum should never be higher on a stave than a side drum. The copyist must make sure that such notation is consistent throughout the part.

Since the percussionist frequently has to move some distance between different instruments, it is common to supply the player with several copies of the same part so that he or she does not have to carry a score from one instrument to another during the piece. This does not mean that page-turns are easier; quite the opposite, in fact, since having moved from one instrument to another and back again, the player may have to turn over several pages to find his or her place. And because the player will nearly always be holding sticks, page-turns need to be organised with extra special care. Bear in mind also that the player may be further away from his or her part than anyone else in the orchestra: changes of instrument should for this reason be particularly clear.

There are around a hundred 'approved' symbols or pictograms representing percussion instruments and stick types, which alone should be sufficient reason for not using them. Whatever their value in a score, it is indisputable that percussionists dislike them intensely, and they should never be used in parts. At a distance of two metres,

 looks much like ,

and no player wants to confuse a motor-horn with side-drum sticks!

All the percussion instruments required by the player must be listed at the beginning of the part, on a separate page if necessary. Pitched percussion should be notated, as in the following list:

PERCUSSION I

Metal sheet
Crash cymbals
Javanese gongs: 

Suspended cymbal
Suspended bell: 

Sleigh bells (set i)
Bell plates: 

Snare drum
Lion's roar

PERCUSSION II

Tam-tam
Sleigh bells (set ii)
Crotales (antique cymbals): 

Suspended bell: 

Glockenspiel
Caribbean steel drums: 

Large bass drum
Contrabass bow

Timpani

Timpani are traditionally separate from the rest of the percussion section and in a full orchestra rarely double with other percussion instruments (although a percussionist may double on a second set of timpani). The composer may specify changes of tuning, for example 'G to A♭' or 'B♭ to B♮'. Tunings of individual drums should be specified at the beginning of the score, as with other pitched percussion not assumed to come in chromatic sets.

Piano, Celesta

Piano parts do not normally require any special treatment, but the celesta will have been transposed an octave down from sounding pitch by the composer. These are doubling instruments; celesta parts should not normally be assigned to percussionists (although some percussionists may be able to double on keyboards if necessary).

Harp

Again, it is the composer's responsibility to organise the harp part, keeping constant track of the pedal positions and marking all changes of pedal. Though such information is not actually necessary in the full score (unlike any other score detail it concerns the player only, not the conductor), the composer should not leave it to the copyist. But the copyist functioning as an editor needs to know the rules.

The harp has seven pedals, one for each note of the octave, and each pedal has three positions; flat, natural and sharp. By depressing the C pedal to the sharp position, all the C strings are sharpened. The bottom C, and usually the D as well, are not affected by the pedal, however, and have to be tuned by hand: this cannot practically be done during a piece. If the harp has a top G, that too may need to be tuned by hand.

The pedals on the instrument are positioned thus (shown from above):

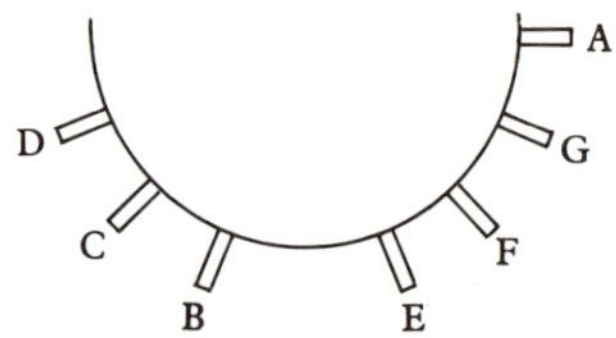

The most convenient way to set out the pedal changes for the player is to order the notes beginning with B, for example as follows:

This may also be set out diagrammatically:

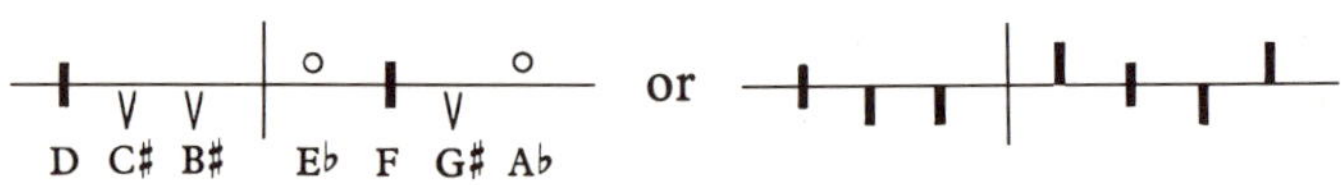

(note that the ordering here is D C B). These diagrams are instantly recognisable to harpists but are rarely used by composers. The symbol ⊕ indicates that the strings should be damped.

The string tuning does not need to be written out in full every time the harp plays. For example, with the pedals set out as above, one might imagine after a few bars an indication to change two pedals; C natural, E sharp, then later G natural. If, after a gap, the harp plays a C major glissando, this could be notated as B♮ (C D) E♮ (F G) A♮; the bracketed notes indicating that they need not be changed. (In music with key signatures, the harpist will automatically tune to the key, and the initial tunings are superfluous.)

Harmonics are notated by a small circle above the note, which indicates that the sound will be an octave higher. Only one harmonic at a time can be played with the right hand, but up to three harmonics in close position may be played with the left hand. Chords must not contain more than four notes to each hand since the little fingers are not used. The stretch from thumb to fourth finger is approxinately a tenth.

Harp music is notated much like piano music, but remember that it cannot be assumed that the right hand is always above the left hand. Nevertheless, the left hand is better positioned to play lower notes.

Because of the nature of harp writing, it is often difficult to know where to place rests; for example, the following passage may be notated in three ways:

Of these, (i) is probably the most commonly used, (ii) correct but pedantic, and (iii) the simplest and clearest. The copyist will need to adapt to the situation.

Guitar

Paper with no more than eight staves should be used, especially for a solo part, since the music is often contrapuntal with tails of the separate voices outward from the stave, and plenty of room needs to be left between the staves for other information:

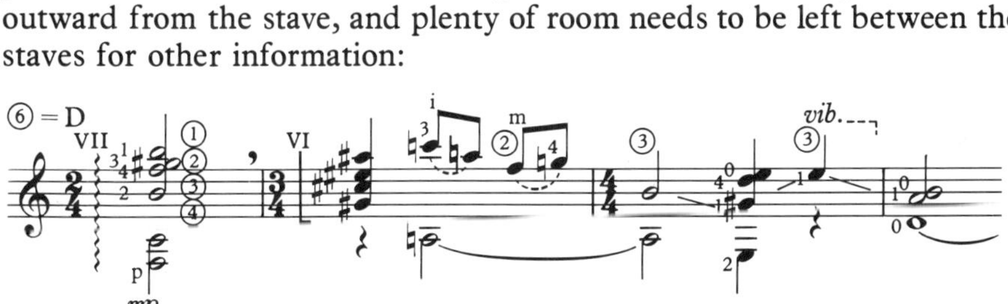

In the example above, roman numerals denote position (or fret), and are written above the stave. Numbers in circles represent string numbers and are placed as near as possible to the notes concerned.

The symbol for *barré* (⌊ or [ ) varies in length depending on the number of strings the first finger of the left hand has to hold down on the fingerboard. The instruction as to which fret to use (I, II, III, IV, etc.) is often shown above the *barré* bracket. Sometimes a B or a C (indicating *barré* or *cejilla*) is added before the roman numerals.

Left-hand fingerings (1, 2, 3, 4) go in front of the notes, and right-hand fingerings (p, i, m, a)* go above or under the notes (and as close to them as possible), except in the case of chords, where the right-hand fingering should be placed either just after or just before the notes, depending on the amount of room. Where no fingering is provided, enough space should be left for the guitarist to add his or her own.

Oblique lines written to the left of the fingering are not glissandi but guide-strokes indicating change of finger position (left hand). These are positioned / or \ as appropriate to show the direction of the change.

Note that the guide-stroke between the last two quavers in the above example is downward.

Technical (*ligado*) slurs are often written as dotted slurs to distinguish them from phrase-marks. They usually go from notehead to notehead (as opposed to being written on the tail side).

Sometimes, the player is required to re-tune the instrument. Unusual string tuning (or *scordatura*) is shown at the beginning of the piece, or movement, above the stave. If the third string is to be re-tuned to F sharp, for example, this will be shown thus:

Rasgueado (flamenco-type strumming) is a commonly-used device created by the strings being hit in rapid succession with the fingernails in the direction shown by the arrow. This effect is different from the ordinary 'spread' chord (*arpeggiando*), so must be distinguished by the abbreviation

*that is, pulgar (thumb), index, medial, annular

'*rasg.*' (or 'R') written above the arrow.

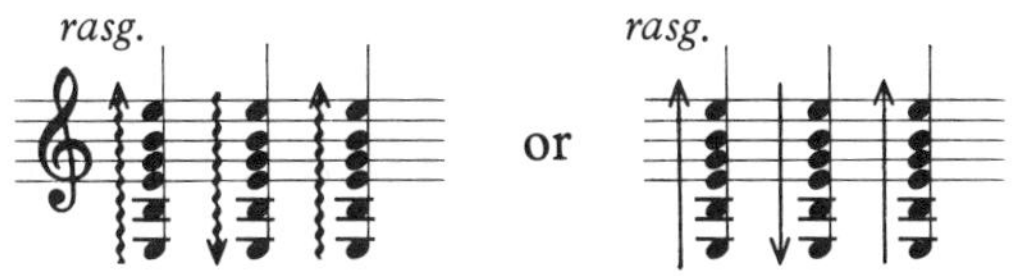

Guitar notation is far from standardised. The guidelines given here follow the recommendations of some of the larger publishing houses and the engravers used by them, and make for a fairly tidy manuscript. There are, however, plenty of well-known guitar editions in which some of the elements are written slightly differently, or are placed in alternative positions.

One area in particular where there is no standardisation, and one which causes some disagreement amongst guitarists, is the notation of harmonics. There are several common (and acceptable) ways of notating both natural and artificial guitar harmonics, but rather than discuss them all, it will suffice here to recommend one good system for each that will cater for most situations and not complicate a score unnecessarily.

A natural harmonic is always written at sounding pitch (or an octave lower with an *8va* sign). The note may be indicated by an ordinary notehead with a small circle above, but if preferred, a lozenge-shaped notehead* has the advantage of being instantly recognisable without requiring the circle (which would add to the peppering of numbers and signs). The string number, encircled, and the fret number (in roman numerals) should be given.

Natural harmonics:

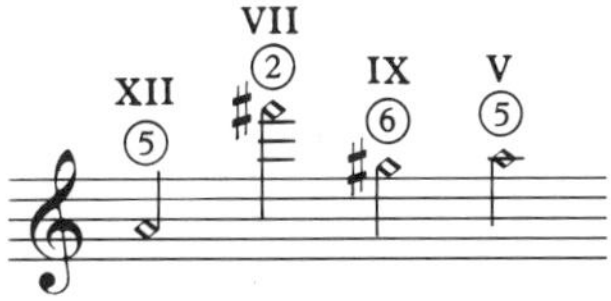

An artificial harmonic is one produced on a string artificially shortened by being stopped with a finger. It is best notated by an ordinary notehead on the note where it is stopped with the left hand, with *art. harm* and *8va* written above. Lozenge-shaped noteheads and circles are unnecessary, although it is quite acceptable to use them (and many guitarists still prefer them, finding them more conspicuous as harmonics). The note will sound

*See page 49, *Noteheads*

an octave higher than the stopping point.

Artificial harmonics:

If the composer is unsure about the way in which a harmonic is to be produced, it is advisable to provide the intended resultant pitch. This should be written after the note as a small unstemmed notehead in brackets.

Take care to distinguish between the sign for a harmonic (a small round ' o ') and that for an open string (an oval '0'), and remember that guitar music is always written an octave higher than it sounds.

Strings

Violins use only the treble clef. Violas play mainly in the alto clef; the treble clef need not be used except where the notes are consistently high.

Cellos remain in the bass clef as much as possible, using the tenor and treble clefs for high passages rather than for isolated notes (unless they are more than three leger lines above the stave). Jumping between clefs should be avoided if possible.

High passages are unusual for the double bass, so the use of clefs other than the bass clef is rare. As with the cello, the tenor and treble clefs may be used if absolutely necessary. Remember that on the double bass all notes, including harmonics, sound an octave lower than written. Some textbooks recommend that harmonics in the treble clef be written at actual pitch but players find this confusing, so this practice should be avoided.

For all the strings, *8va* markings (to indicate an octave higher) are used only in the treble clef, and then sparingly.

A common area of notational ambiguity is that of string harmonics, especially natural harmonics. Below are five ways of notating the same note on the violin, involving three methods of producing the harmonic:

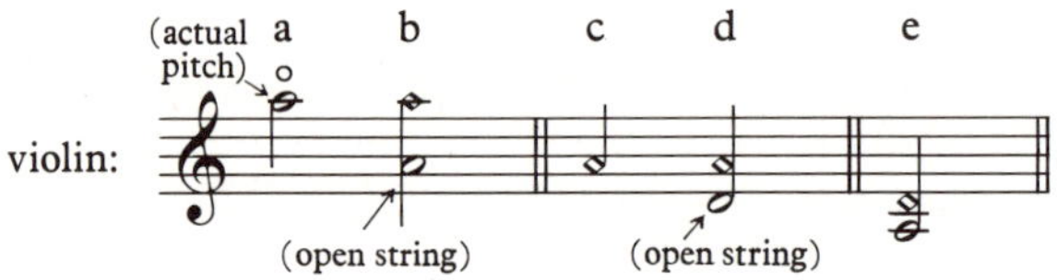

If (a) is used, the player will assume that an octave harmonic (that is, sounding an octave higher than the open string) is intended. The figure II for the A string could be added, but the notation at (b) is superfluous. (c) and (d) are a fifth harmonic on the D string; (c) is technically more correct since the D is not actually fingered and does not need to be written down; but since the lozenge notehead alone cannot indicate the duration of the note, the open string is needed to show this, as at (d). (e) is the only correct way of notating an artificial harmonic as both pitches must be written down.

Harmonic circles need only be written above octave harmonics. For other harmonics, it can be helpful to indicate the resultant pitch in brackets as below. It is much more important for the player to know what note is intended than how the composer wishes or hopes it to be realised. Some composers add the harmonic circle above all harmonics, but this is not necessary.

violin: 

Distinguish carefully between o for harmonics and 0 for open strings:

in a violin part could easily be misinterpreted.

(See also page 44, *Divisi*.)

iv. Problematic Areas

Accidentals

It is worth remembering that players tend to be a good deal less worried about accidentals than composers, and prefer to see a part uncluttered by perhaps unnecessary symbols.

Composers vary greatly in their use of accidentals. The Schoenbergian method of applying an accidental to every note is, in instrumental parts, unnecessarily fussy, and should be edited by the copyist. The extreme to which this is occasionally taken, for example as here:

should not be transferred to the parts. Many composers apply accidentals to notes tied across the bar. This can be disconcerting to the score reader who may think that either the previous accidental was misread, or else it was an error. Obviously, this too is a practice that should not be transferred to the parts. If, however, after such an instance the same pitch is reiterated in the bar, the accidental must be repeated. When a note is tied over to a new system, the accidentals should be repeated in brackets.

The two examples below show how the composer's notation might be changed in the part. In example (i), inessential accidentals are marked a; reminder accidentals are marked b; all others are essential. In example (ii), reminder accidentals appear in brackets. In some cases parenthetic accidentals might be regarded as mere pedantry; here, however, the low G in the second bar has a natural sign in brackets because it might otherwise be taken as a misreading for G sharp; and an unbracketed accidental might lead a player to think he or she had earlier played a wrong note. The accidental applying to the final G sharp is essential: unless the music is diatonic, grace-note accidentals should not be taken as holding good throughout the bar. Were the final note here a G natural, it would be necessary to add the natural sign.

i)
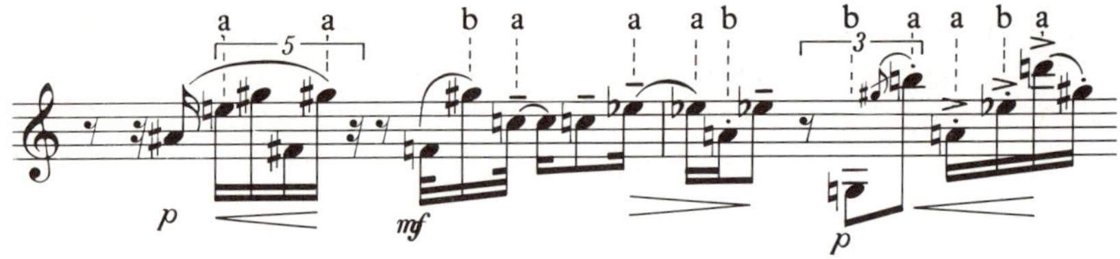

ii)

When copying a part where the composer has put two instruments on one line, care must be taken to ensure that the right accidentals apply. The second flute part extracted from the example below must appear as in (b), not as in (a).

Flutes I & II
(full score)

a)  b) 

The notation of quartertones is, unfortunately, not yet entirely standardised. All the following examples are common.

 = a quarter-tone sharp  = a quarter-tone flat

 = three quarter-tones sharp  = three quarter-tones flat

Whatever notation the composer has adopted in the score should be used in the parts, with an explanatory footnote.

Editing

Throughout this manual it is pointed out that the copyist must do more than merely copy, and several instances are shown where the notation in the score needs to be altered in some way to be suitable for the part.

Some notation is aimed more specifically at helping the score-reader than the player, and the copyist must learn to recognise such areas where editing is appropriate for the parts. In the James Dillon example on page 43, the beaming of notes across bar lines makes the full score easier to read than conventional rhythmic grouping would.

The individual parts, however, are much better notated as shown:

oboe: 

There may well be occasions when the composer objects to a copyist's taking such liberties, though, and however sensible the solution may seem from a player's point of view, to the composer it may not be acceptable.

A common area of contention is that of enharmonic changes made in transposition. The copyist may think it best to change the spelling when transposing an example such as the following (i), for B flat clarinet. The copyist's version (ii) is easier to read than a literal translation of the accidentals (iii):

i) 

ii) 

iii) 

Yet some composers might regard such alterations as being detrimental to inherent tonal or harmonic implications. It is as well to consult the composer before tampering with *any* aspect of the notation that might be (at least to the composer!) conceptually important to the piece.

Divisi

Divisi (usually shortened to *div.*) should always be cancelled by *unisono* (*unis.*). Where *divisi* is indicated in string parts, how the desks divide is up to the players but the copyist must be aware of some basic rules. *Divisi* must be indicated each time it occurs; in some instances it can otherwise be difficult to distinguish between *divisi* and double stopping. Unless a *divisi a 2* part is easily readable from one stave, it should be copied onto two separate staves. If only one stave is used, the stems must be placed in opposite directions. The players will normally divide at the desk, with the outside (first) players playing the top line, and the inside players the lower.

Divisi a 3 can present problems, depending on the number of players. If there are twelve, they can divide either two desks to a part or, for better balance, by player, with the top part being taken by the first, fourth, seventh and tenth players, and so on. If possible, the part should be written on three separate staves, but if there is not room, two parts will have to go on one stave, with the stems placed in opposite directions.

For *divisi a 4*, the players will normally divide at the desk, with the part written on two or four staves. If there is a long section in which the parts are too complex to go onto two staves, there will inevitably be problems with page-turns. One solution to this (though best avoided) is to make different

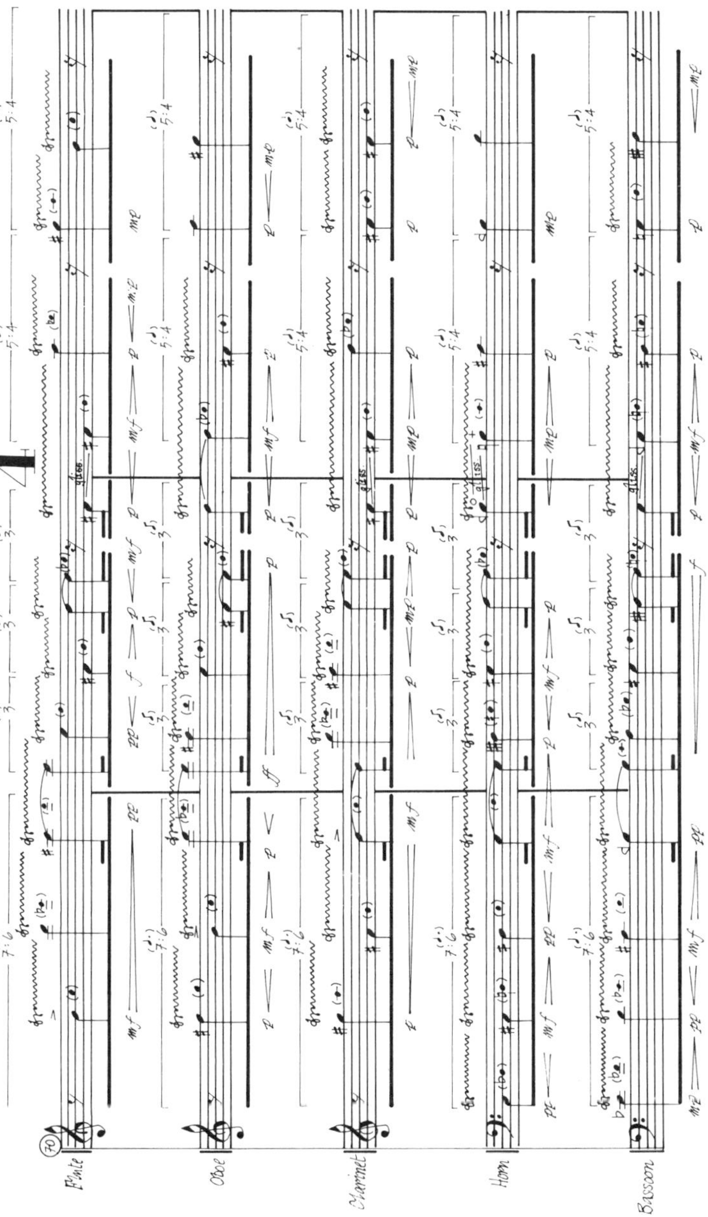

From the full score of *Le Rivage* by James Dillon. This score is a facsimile of the composer's handwritten manuscript.

parts; one for the first and second line, and the other for the third and fourth. Care must be taken with layout both before and after the *divisi,* so that the player can see clearly which part he or she is to play. Other more elaborate *divisi* may make it essential that more than one part be made for each string section.

Where a string section divides between one solo player or more and the other strings, the parts are marked as *solo* (or *soli* if plural) and *gli altri* ('the others').

Page-turns must be avoided altogether in active divisi sections.

IV. NOTATION, STYLE AND ORTHOGRAPHY

Clarity of image: general

In almost any printing process apart from lithography (which is too expensive for the purpose of producing most orchestral or ensemble performing material), black lines increase in thickness (provided they are thick or opaque enough to be registered by the printing machine), whereas white gaps tend to shrink; thus black lines close together will sometimes merge on the printed copy.

Full scores may sometimes need to be reduced in size from the original. If the image to be printed is not consistently clear and sharp, there will be problems: when the image is reduced, the eye will see any blurring effects to be exaggerated. Bear this in mind particularly when writing accidentals, 'white' notes and multiple beams; and remember that the presence of stave lines will further reduce clarity when they interrupt white spaces. Make sure:

i) that accidentals are wide enough to be clear in any printed copy:

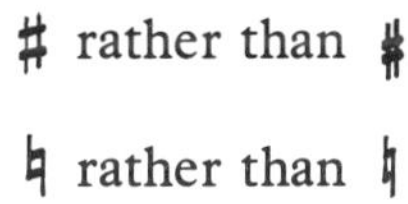

ii) that semibreves, minims, harmonic or other white noteheads are clear enough not to 'fill in':

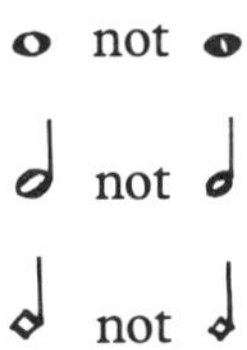

iii) that multiple beams are not so close together that they could merge at any point:

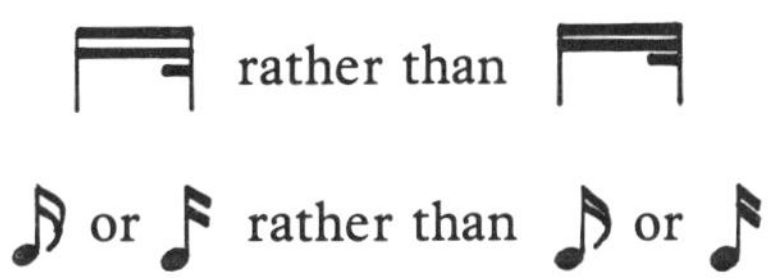

Beams (especially multiple beams), when positioned within or partly within the stave, should be placed so that the white spaces between them conflict as little as possible with the stave lines:

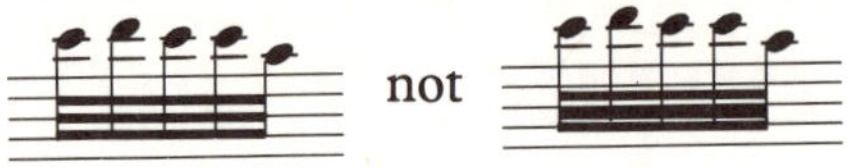

The second example when reproduced may suffer a 'wedging' effect between the beams and the stave lines. It is of course more important to be able to see the beams than any stave lines they might obscure, so all beams must be noticeably thicker.

Clefs

Clefs should be carefully drawn, as in the examples below. For the sake of clarity, personal idiosyncrasies of style should be avoided; clefs should be drawn in the standard way:

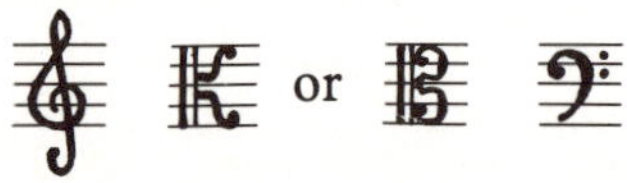

Dry transfers (for example, Notaset) are occasionally used for clefs to give an otherwise hand-drawn score a more polished appearance (see page 14, *Dry transfers*), but many publishers dislike them because of their tendency to become detached from the page.

Changes of clef in the full score should not automatically be transferred to the parts. The composer may, for example, have put a bassoon part into the tenor clef simply to avoid its colliding with a low bass clarinet in the score. If a bassoon chord is notated in the full score thus,

it would be absurd to put the second player's part into the tenor clef merely because the first player's part has to be. It is up to the copyist to work out in such cases which clef is most suitable for the player.

When a clef changes within a part, a smaller clef should be used, as near to the first note in the new clef as is possible without interfering with any rests, or just before the last bar line if the change comes with a new stave. In parts for sessions or film scores, it is common for the clef (and key signature) to be put at the beginning of the part and never repeated. This practice should be avoided as it can be annoying for the players not to have all the information in front of them.

Noteheads

Crotchet and quaver noteheads should be slightly oval, and large enough to fill the space between stave lines. Minim noteheads are slightly wider than black noteheads, and should be 'shaded' as illustrated below to make them instantly clear. Semibreves are slightly wider still, and are shaded on the opposite sides from minim noteheads:

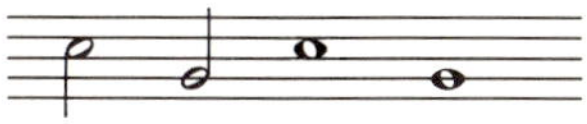 not 

Breves may be notated in three ways:

 or  or 

If the first or second symbols are chosen, the number of verticals should be consistent with the notation used for breve rests, if they appear in the same work.

Where harmonics are notated by single lozenge-shaped noteheads, filled-in lozenges may be used for 'black' notes (crotchets and notes of lesser value), while hollow lozenges are reserved for 'white' notes (minims and notes of greater value), to avoid confusion between rhythmic values. Hollow lozenges should always be shaded as shown here to make them easily recognisabe:

When harmonics notated with both an ordinary notehead and a lozenge are tied, it is customary to connect only the ordinary notehead with a tie, and not the lozenge. This may not seem logical, but is nevertheless standard practice. Augmentation dots are not usually added to the lozenge either.

Stems

Stems must be vertical, and should touch the head at the corner:

 not 

and should not extend too far above or below the notehead. The engraver's rule is that the stem should normally extend to the space of an octave (provided there is only one part on the stave), unless, of course, it is part of a beamed group of widely-spaced notes such as that shown below, or unless it is the stem of a note beyond the first leger line either above or below the stave. In the case of notes further out from the stave than this, the tail-ends of minim, crotchet and quaver stems should not normally reach beyond the middle stave line. Stems of notes with more than one flag or beam extend a little further.

Where there are two or more parts on the stave, stems extending in what would otherwise be the 'wrong' direction should not protrude too far above or below the stave. Stems of high notes in the upper part and low notes in the lower part will be less than an octave space in length:

There is no absolute rule for stem direction within a group of notes and composers cannot be relied upon to follow any particular system. The copyist should develop a visual sense of what looks right, bearing in mind that stem direction is largely determined by the placing of the majority of noteheads (within a group) above or below the central stave line. The highest or lowest note is often the determinant, irrespective of the majority of notes. The examples below give some guidelines.

The stem of an unbeamed note on the middle line of the stave will normally extend downwards but, again, a majority rule applies. Some engravers follow a rule that in a $\frac{4}{4}$ or $\frac{6}{4}$ bar, the stem of a note on the middle line follows the direction of the other stem or stems in the same half of the bar within reason (in a $\frac{3}{2}$ bar this would apply to each third of the bar):

Chords are more straightforward: if the distribution of notes is more heavily weighted above the middle line the stem will go down, and vice-versa:

Normal stemming rules are not applicable either to cues (see page 29) or to grace-notes (see page 58).

Chords

Chords and clusters notated according to traditional engraving rules are far easier to read than if they are copied regardless of the conventions concerning positioning of noteheads on the stems, and alignment.

In order to accommodate two notes forming an interval of a second on the same stem, it is necessary to displace one of them to the 'wrong' side of the stem. The upper of two such adjacent noteheads will go to the right of the stem, and the lower to the left, regardless of stem direction:

If there are other notes in the chord, they will be placed as normal according to the stem direction, as shown. Where an odd number of notes forms a cluster, the majority of the notes are arranged on what would normally be the 'correct' side of the stem. Thus in a three-note cluster, the notehead to be displaced will be the one in the middle, in order for the other two to be placed in their normal position:

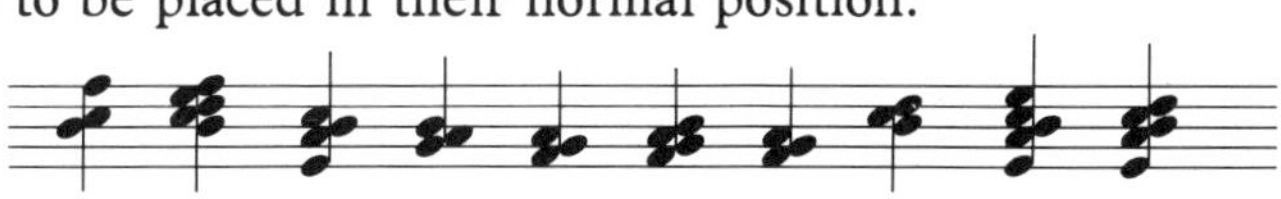

In a chord where two noteheads with different accidentals must share a stem and also a line or space, but cannot be placed either side of the stem because one of them would interfere with adjacent notes, it is modern practice to place the two companion noteheads side by side on the appropriate side of the stem, so that the one nearer the stem is attached as normal and the other one is connected to the main stem by a short oblique extension stem, as shown here:

When aligning chords in separate parts or on separate staves, the noteheads to align are those which are on the 'normal' side of the stem (not the ones that are displaced). All these rules apply equally to semibreves and other stemless notes; they should be positioned as they would be if they were stemmed:

Positioning of accidentals before chords

Engravers have detailed rules for grouping accidentals in certain combinations, the aim being to use the space on the stave as tidily and as economically as possible. The following guidelines should be borne in mind.

Where two accidentals are too close to be aligned with each other (that is, less than a seventh apart), the higher one will be placed nearer the note:

Likewise, where there are several in very close position, they will be placed further away from the notes as they descend, unless in a widely extending chord there is room for another to slot in closer to the note:

A pair of accidentals as far apart as a seventh or more should be vertically aligned.

Slurs

Unless all stems within a phrase extend upwards, the slur should, wherever practical, be placed on the upper side. This applies even when only one stem is down:

Where there are two or more voices on the stave, slurs are placed on the outside, near the stems rather than near the noteheads*:

Special attention must be paid to string slurs, which determine bowing. The composer should be precise about this, bearing in mind that to a string player (though not necessarily to a wind or brass player) there is a great deal of difference between

 and 

If there is any ambiguity, the copyist should consult the composer or publisher.

Ties

Ties always go from notehead to notehead (though without touching them), even when the note is dotted, and even when there is more than one voice on the stave. Where there is a single voice, ties connecting notes with downward stems are placed above the noteheads, and ties connecting notes with upward stems are placed below the noteheads. Where notes with stems in opposite directions are tied, the tie will be placed above.

Where there are two or more voices, ties will always be placed on the outside (that is, on the same side as the stems):

Be careful not to place ties where they could be confused with stave lines, or where they might obscure augmentation dots:

 not 

*Except in guitar music (see page 38)

Articulation marks

So long as there is only one voice on the stave, slurs, ties, most accents and staccato dots should always be placed near the notehead and in the next clear space between stave lines as illustrated below. If the note is on a line, neither these nor any other markings (harmonic circles, etc.) should share a space with half a notehead!

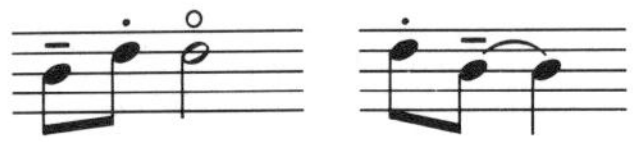

not

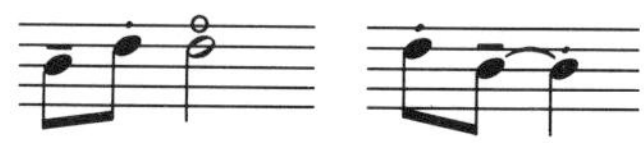

Where there are multiple accents as in the next example, a staccato dot or dash will be closest to the notehead, followed by a tenuto marking above or below according to stem direction. Other accents will follow in order of intensity, as in these (extreme) examples, so that the weakest is always nearest the notehead:

If there is more than one voice on the stave, all these markings are displaced to the stem side, directly above or below the note, but in the same order of proximity to the note as they would follow as single voices:

British and European engravers usually centre displaced staccatos and staccatissimo dots and dashes above the notehead rather than above the stem (as often seen in American scores). If a slur or a tie is involved, staccato dots and dashes will in most circumstances be placed between the notehead and the slur or tie, while other accents will go outside it:

Exceptions to the rule are shown in the following examples, where to observe it would be untidy:

not

Tenuto markings applying to repeated notes with slurs should be placed between the notehead and the slur to avoid confusion with ties:

The symbol for natural harmonics (o) and bowing marks (V ⊓) always remain above the notes, irrespective of stem direction. Bowing marks are placed above the harmonic circle, and if there are accents, slurs or ties above the notehead, the harmonic sign will go above them:

violin: 

String indications for open strings (0) and numerals (I, II, III, IV) are generally placed near the noteheads as shown above, rather than near the stem. Be careful to draw all these markings clearly. Staccato dots must be quite bold and clearly distinguishable from staccatissimo dashes, and tenuto markings should be positioned clear of stave lines and leger lines.

Augmentation dots

Like staccato dots, these must be bold enough to be immediately obvious. An augmentation dot will normally be placed in the centre of the space above the notehead to which it applies, whether or not the note is in a space or on a line, and regardless of stem direction. This applies also to notes with leger lines.

 not 

Where there is more than one voice on the stave, and the augmentation dot applies to a note on a line, the dot is placed on the side on which the stems of that voice extend:

Dots applying to intervals of a second are placed as follows:

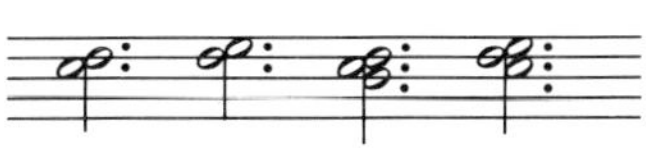

Leger lines

These should be the same distance apart as the existing stave lines, but are normally drawn slightly thicker. When working on transparency, it is helpful to have a sheet of the same manuscript paper underneath. Using this as a guide, noteheads in an extended passage of high or low notes may be written out before the leger lines are drawn.

Rests

Rests must be carefully drawn, and positioned correctly on the stave:

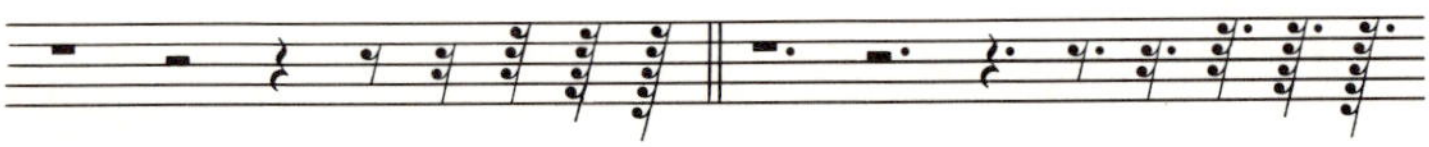

Hand-copied rests should be drawn as illustrated here in 'engraved style', as favoured by publishers. There are different ways of drawing crotchet rests (and), but these are not so easily recognisable as the one shown in the example above and players always prefer the notation they are most familiar with.

The breve rest may be notated in three ways:

(but see page 49, *Noteheads*).

As well as being used to represent a rest twice as long as a semibreve, and a whole bar's rest (in bars of greater value than a semibreve), the breve rest, with a fermata above it, is sometimes used as an indeterminately long rest in *senza misura* passages.

All rests must be placed at the beginning of the value they represent, unless they are either semibreve or breve rests which are centred on the bar when applied as whole-bar rests (see example below). If a semibreve rest is used to indicate four crotchet beats but not a whole bar, however, this too must be placed at the beginning of the value it represents and not in the middle of the bar. Similarly, if the value of a breve rest does not constitute a whole bar, the rest is placed at the beginning of the value.

Traditional engraving practice provides strict rules about the notation of rests in various meters. These rules are designed to clarify the division of beats and aid distinction between, for example, compound and simple meters. The rules as adhered to conscientiously by the best engravers are unnecessarily detailed for the purpose of this manual but the aim of such rules should be borne in mind by the copyist when faced with a choice of notation.

Composers are often careless about the grouping of rests in full scores, and it will help the player if the copyist arranges the notation to suit the way in which the player will think through them. It should not be assumed, however, that an unconventional division of beats in a part is necessarily wrong. The copyist must study the rest of that section of the full score to see how the music in all the other parts is grouped. These days, a 6/8 bar, for example, does not necessarily have an implied division of 3 + 3. The composer may intend the division to be, say, 2 + 3 + 1, in which case the rests must match. (Strictly, conducting signs – see page 60 – should be used as well to make the divisions quite clear.)

Multiple rests

The traditional method of indicating more than one bar's rest by blocks is preferable to the use of one thick line for all numbers, except in percussion parts where on a single-line stave blocks are impractical. Block symbols are drawn as follows:

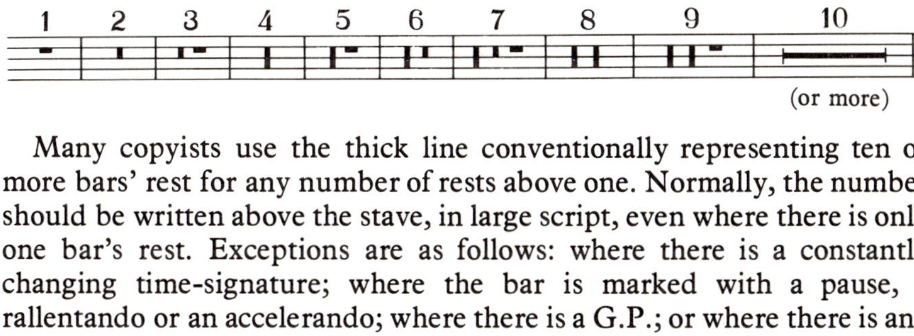

Many copyists use the thick line conventionally representing ten or more bars' rest for any number of rests above one. Normally, the number should be written above the stave, in large script, even where there is only one bar's rest. Exceptions are as follows: where there is a constantly changing time-signature; where the bar is marked with a pause, a rallentando or an accelerando; where there is a G.P.; or where there is any other distinguishing feature such as a cue. (For the placing of rests with cues, see page 28.)

It is helpful to the performer if some spatial differentiation is made between short and long rests, as in the following example:

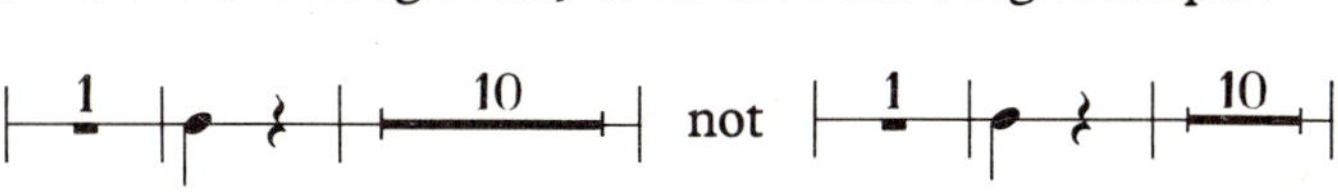

If an instrument does not play again after a specific point in a work or movement, then '*tacet al fine*' may be used. '*Tacet*' should also be used if an instrument is silent for a whole movement. It must never be used for rests *during* a movement if the instrument is to play again.

Grace-notes

The noteheads of these should be visibly smaller than ordinary notes, but not too small to be clear. Acciaccaturas and notes to be played 'as fast as possible' are usually indicated by a small line through the tail:

It is usual to keep all grace-note stems up; they are, however, sometimes more easily distinguished if their stems are drawn in different directions from those of the notes to which they apply.

Rhythmic irrationals

The positioning of rhythmic irrationals is often problematic, especially if multiple irrationals are used. Traditionally, irrationals applying to beamed groups are written next to the beams, rather than the noteheads:

but if they are bracketed, it is better to write them above the stave. Of the following two examples, a) is easier to read than b):

a)

b)

Brackets (┌─3─┐, ┌─7:6─┐ etc.) should only be used for 'incomplete' irrational groups, or for multiple irrationals. If the first and last notes of a group are joined by a beam, the bracket is not strictly necessary but it may be helpful to apply brackets to long groups.

Repeat bars

The practice of using shorthand signs to indicate repeat bars has become a convention in film and session work, but occasionally it is useful in classical or contemporary music too.

The symbols 𝄎 and 𝄏 should be used only for a series of whole bars; not for anything less than a bar. If a repeated figuration appears in a score notated like this,

it should be written out in long-hand in the part. If the repetition is for one bar only, that bar should be written out in full, but repeat marks may be used for two or more bars. The number of repeats should be written above the stave in small figures, with '1' applying to the first bar:

If a simple two-bar figure is repeated, the abbreviation 𝄏 may be used as shown:

Written instructions

Except in vocal parts, or where there is more than one instrumental voice on a stave, dynamics and expression marks are written below the stave, preferably in italic script. Instructions as to the method of playing (arco, pizz., col legno etc.) go above the stave, preferably in roman script. Tempo directions (always above the stave) must be placed higher, and should be bold. Markings should be aligned where possible, so that instructions are easily distinguished from one another:

not:

Symbols for methods of playing (other than the traditional symbols) should be avoided, as should percussion pictograms; players dislike them intensely. Performers often use ┌┬┐ and └┴┘ for mute on and mute off, but it is up to them to put this into the part, not the copyist, who should always use the conventional written terms (*con sord.* and *senza sord.*).

Conducting signs

If the composer has used conducting signs in the score (such as, for a $\frac{5}{8}$ bar, △, ⊓, 3 + 2 or ♩. ♩ written over the stave), they should also be written in the part. If such indications have not been included in the full score, it may sometimes be helpful if the copyist adds (3 + 2) above the time signature, or even a dotted bar line as a visual aid to complicated rhythms where the division of the beats could be made clearer.

V. FURTHER INFORMATION AND EXAMPLES

Further sources of reference

The professional engraver or processor who intends to produce first-class work without the assistance of a high-quality computerised engraving system will need to know detailed rules about spacing and other aspects of graphics that are not fully described in this volume. Recommended reference books which provide such information are as follows:

Ted Ross, *The Art of Music Engraving and Processing*; Hansen (Miami, 1970)

Kurt Stone, *Music Notation in the Twentieth Century*; Norton (New York, 1980)

Copying and engraving examples

Much may be learned by anyone interested in music notation and graphics from studying well-originated scores produced by reputable publishers.

Here are presented some single-page examples from scores published fairly recently, using various methods of engraving, processing or copying.

Opposite:

From the vocal score of *Death in Venice* by Benjamin Britten, with piano reduction by Colin Matthews. This score is plate-engraved by the traditional method.

Trav.
and de - light)
und doch schön!)
a sud-den pre-da-to-ry gleam,
ein jä-her raub-tier-haf-ter Schein,
bsn.
pp cresc.
cl.
(tomtoms)
ASCHENBACH
17
mf
What is this urge that fills my tired heart,
Was für ein Drang er - füllt mein müdes Herz,
the crouching ti - ger's
des schlau-en Ti - gers
eyes. Mar - vels un - fold!
Blick. Wun - der rings - um!
hn.
f dim.
p
timp.
mf (with drums as before)
mp
Asch.
this urge that fills my ti-red heart, my ti-red heart,
welch Drang er - füllt mein müdes Herz, mein müdes Herz,
dim.
Mar - vels un - fold! Mar - vels un -
Wun - der rings - um! Wun - der rings -
mf
hn. pp
bsn. pp
p
dim.
pp

197
Piccs.
Fl.
Ob.
E♭ Cl.
B. Cl.
Bsn.
Hns.
Tpts.

From the full score of the opera *New Year* by Michael Tippett. This score is hand-copied, with clefs, accidentals (and time signatures) applied by dry transfer.

From the full score of *Messagesquisse* for seven cellos by Pierre Boulez. This score is hand-copied, with clefs applied by dry transfer.

From 'To the Queen of my Heart' by Frederick Delius, originated by the Halstan process. This method involves the filling in of specially-designed stencilled note-shapes by inked brushes, and ordinary pen-work. The word underlay is typeset and pasted in. The finished artwork, which is one-and-a-half times the intended size when printed, is then reduced by photography.

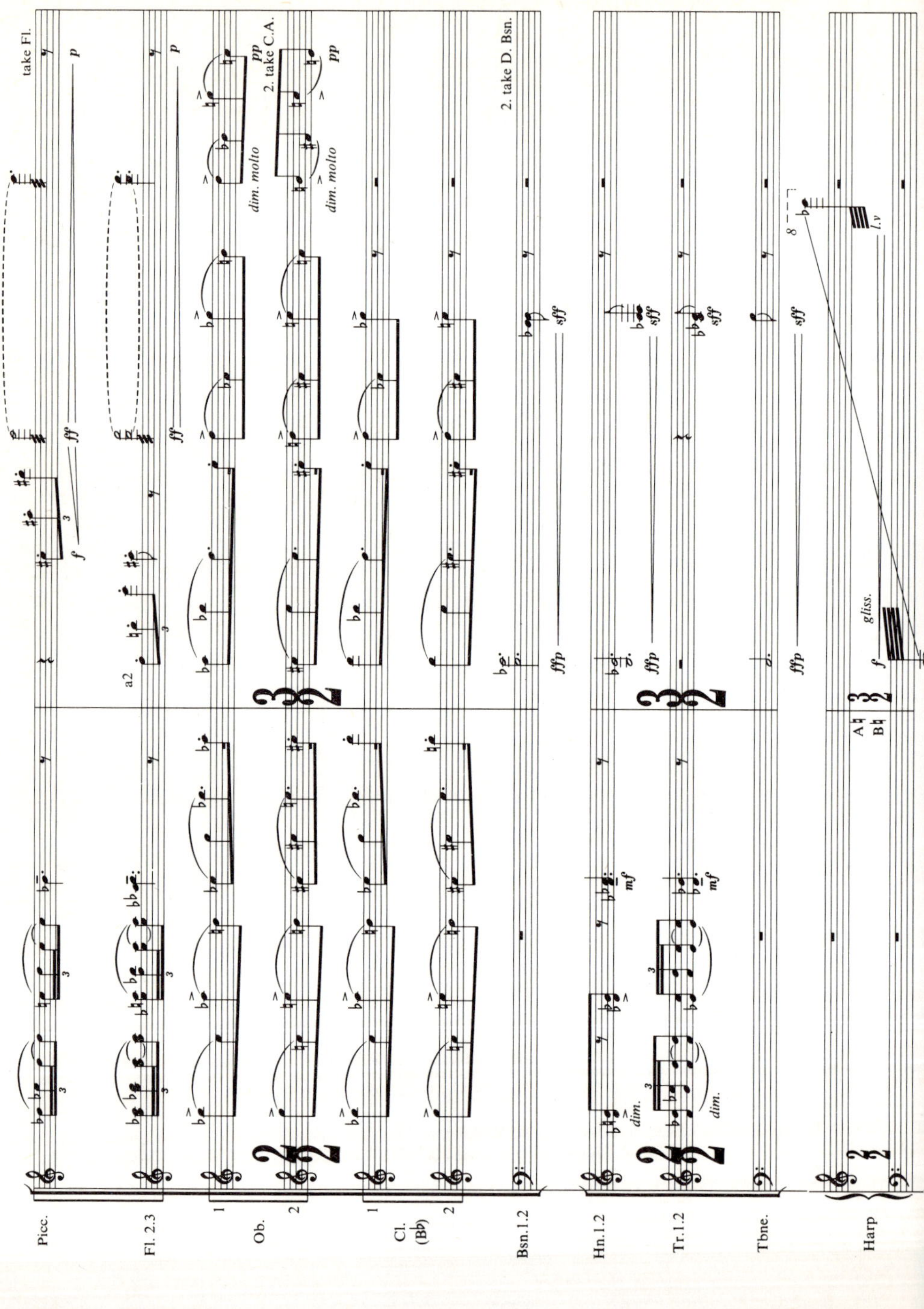
Picc.
Fl. 2.3
Ob.
Cl. (B♭)
Bsn.1.2
Hn.1.2
Tr.1.2
Tbne.
Harp
take Fl.
a2
dim. molto
2. take C.A.
2. take D. Bsn.
dim.
gliss.
l.v

From the full score of *Scenes from Schumann* by Robin Holloway.
This score was processed on a computerised origination system.

From the cello part of the Sonata for Violoncello and Piano by Alexander Goehr. This score is hand-processed using a combination of dry transfers and ink.

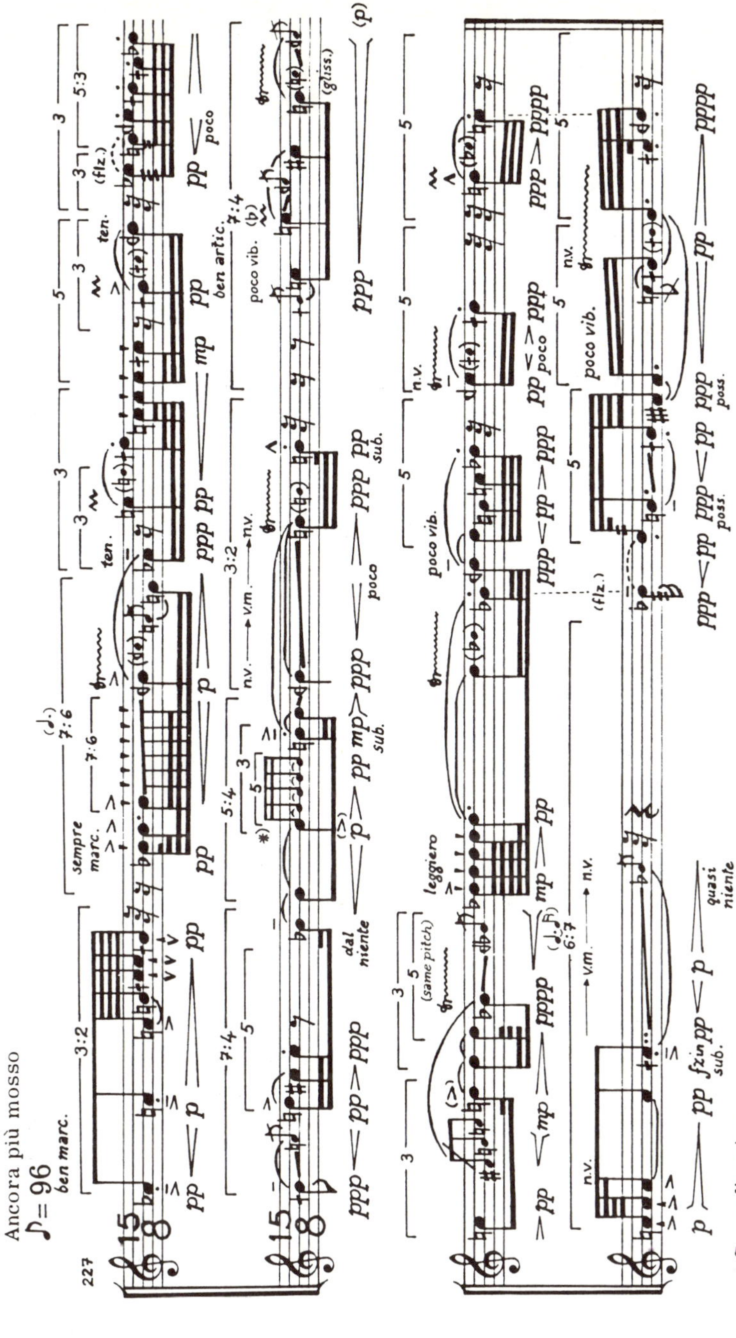

*) Change fingerings

From the horn parts of *Carceri d'Invenzione II* by Brian Ferneyhough. This part is hand-copied, with clefs applied by dry transfer.

Music examples within the text were processed by Michael Langham Rowe. Engravers, processors or copyists of other (full-page) examples are listed as follows.

page 63	*Britten:*	*Jack Thompson*
pages 64–65	*Tippett:*	*Paul Broom*
page 66	*Boulez:*	*Krystyna Reeder*
page 67	*Delius:*	*Halstan & Co. Ltd.*
pages 68–69	*Holloway:*	*Barnes Music Engraving Ltd.*
page 70	*Goehr:*	*Jim Cormack*
page 71	*Ferneyhough:*	*Susan Homewood*

Cover photographs (upper): *Malcolm Crowthers*
(lower): *John Carewe*

Typeset and printed by Halstan & Co. Ltd., Amersham, Bucks.